I dedicate this book to the King who came to His people, but they did not know Him. His story is far greater than any I could ever tell.

I write because I seek to be like the Greatest Storyteller there ever was. Thank you to my Heavenly Father, who, because of His Son Jesus, has now written me into His story forever!

This book and all that I ever do is only for You, my audience of One.

Love always,
Your daughter

www.mascotbooks.com

The Rumble Hunters

©2020 Courtney B. Dunlap. All Rights Reserved. No part of this
publication may be reproduced, stored in a retrieval system or transmitted
in any form by any means electronic, mechanical, or photocopying,
recording or otherwise without the permission of the author.

Second printing. This Mascot Books edition printed in 2019.

For more information, please contact:
Mascot Books
620 Herndon Parkway, Suite 320
Herndon, VA 20170
info@mascotbooks.com

Library of Congress Control Number: 2019903722

CPSIA Code: PRT1219B
ISBN-13: 978-1-64307-120-6

Printed in the United States

THE RUMBLE HUNTERS

WRITTEN BY
COURTNEY B. DUNLAP
ILLUSTRATED BY NAZAR HOROKHIVSKYI

Is that a rumbling in my ear?
A midnight grumbling coming near.
I hope it's not a scaly beast
That wants me for its next great feast.

I check my fish — he's had a fright.
"Don't worry Blue, we'll be all right."
And though he's green around the gills,
He seems to like these nighttime thrills.

We set off quick to search the place.
We'll hunt this sound — we're on the case!
The shadows through an ancient arch
Will lead us to what's in the dark.

I slow my step, try not to trip,
My heartbeat takes another skip.
We creep into the laundry room
And then we hear a sudden boom!

The whirling washer hums and moans.
While belting out odd clanging tones.
With lots of gurgles and a slosh,
It seems the grumble's not the wash.

We won't be playing hide and seek
With any grumbling, furry sneak!
We must be brave as we trek on
And catch this thing before the dawn.

I peek into my lizard's cage,
To try to get a better gauge.
I thought he might have been what thumped,
But no, he's fine. Rex just looks stumped.

We probably have to set a snare,
To lure this dragon from its lair.
I hold the cage and fish bowl tight,
Then journey on through more dim light.

UMPH! THUMP! CRACK!

WHOA! What was that?

I think I squished my doggy's back!

He's shaking as he slips away!

His fur's a blur, but he's okay.

I really hope he comes along,

'Cause old Bear's ears just can't go wrong.

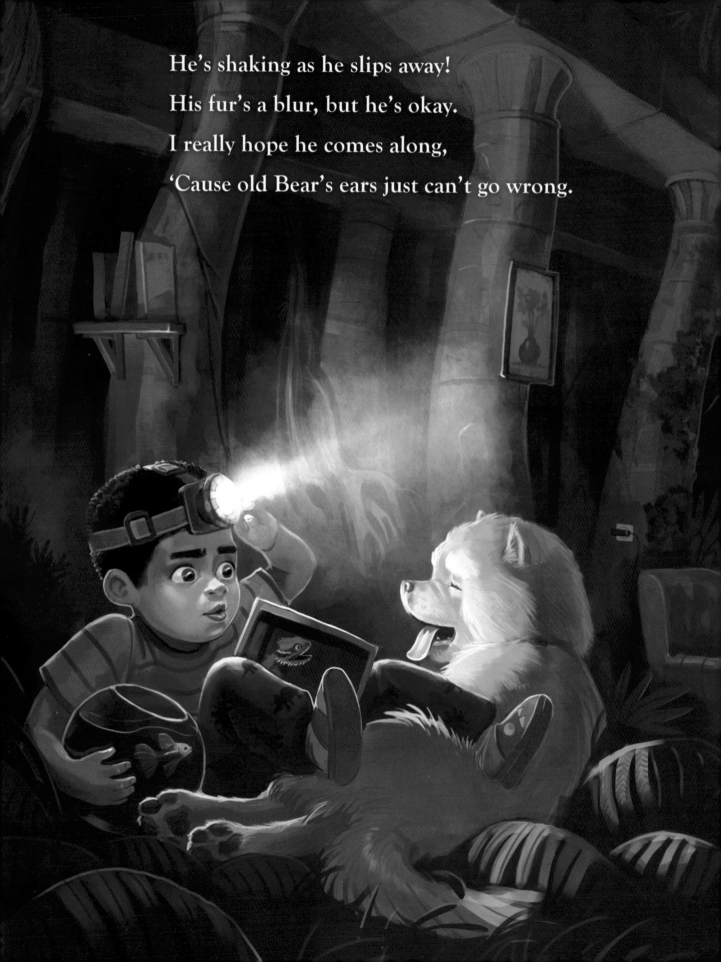

We give a sigh and loudly grunt.

This night looks grim for our big hunt.

Wait, over there! The sliding door!

Whatever lurks can't beat us four!

We listen close for each new howl
And stalk our prey just like an owl.
It seems this is our biggest foe,
I think I'll call in my big bro!

We need his help before day breaks —
I know Eli's got what it takes!
We search the place with great concern.
No pillow, blanket left unturned.

It sounds as if Thor's hammer fell!
But where it is, I just can't tell.
It might be here! Or over there!
It really could be anywhere!

Each clamor's simply not the same.
I'm tired of this listening game!
We vow to scour and must go on
To catch this snarling, spewing spawn.

We'll chase it to that tall bookcase
Or trap it in our small crawl space.
Because that rumbling, grumbling sound
Is somewhere close—it's almost found!

And now we hear a tiny peep.
It's from our sis who's not asleep.
Naomi rubs her aching eyes.
We bring her, too, to shush her cries.

"Now hold on guys, wait up one sec!
There's one more hall we didn't check."
Each rumble warms our hunting trail,
Because we know our ears can't fail.

This nighttime quest with our brave six

A splashing, crawling, walking mix.

This last room surely has some clues.

We hold our breath and stand in twos.

Our parents' door is closed up tight,
But that won't stop this thrilling night.
We push and push and then we're through,
But what we hear sounds like a zoo!

To our surprise what sounds like roars
Is actually from our dad who snores!
He's shaking ceilings, floors, and walls,
And resonating down the halls.

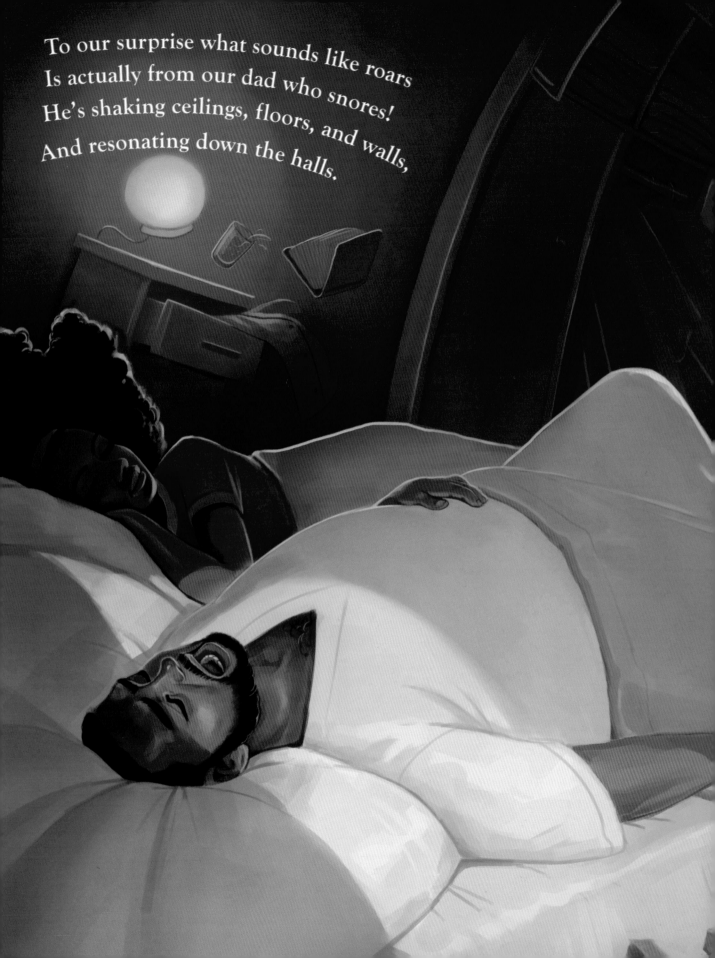

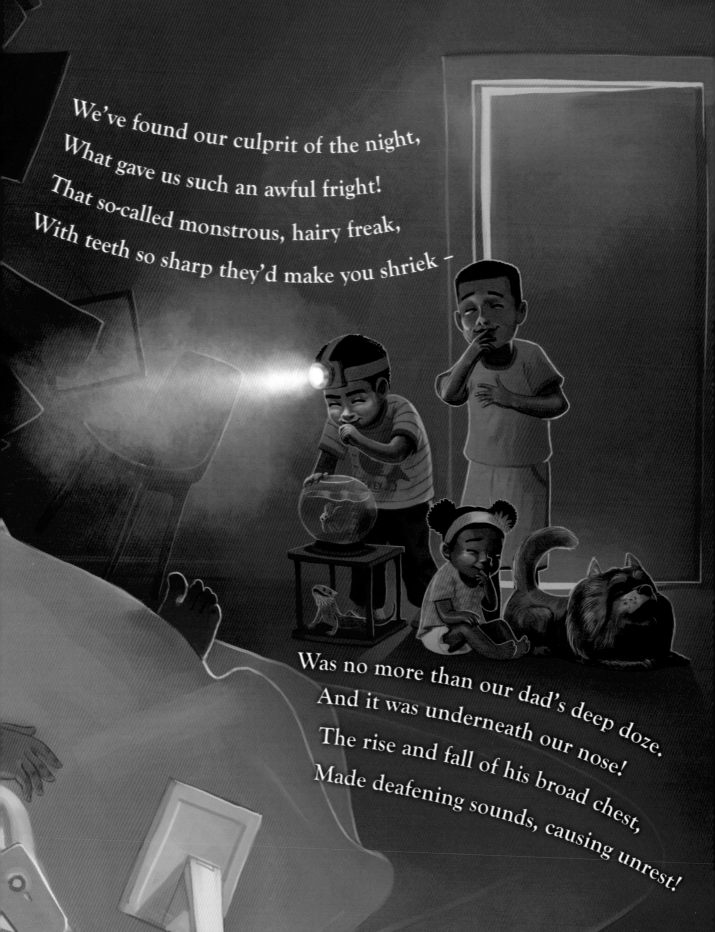

We've found our culprit of the night,
What gave us such an awful fright!
That so-called monstrous, hairy freak,
With teeth so sharp they'd make you shriek –

Was no more than our dad's deep doze.
And it was underneath our nose!
The rise and fall of his broad chest,
Made deafening sounds, causing unrest!

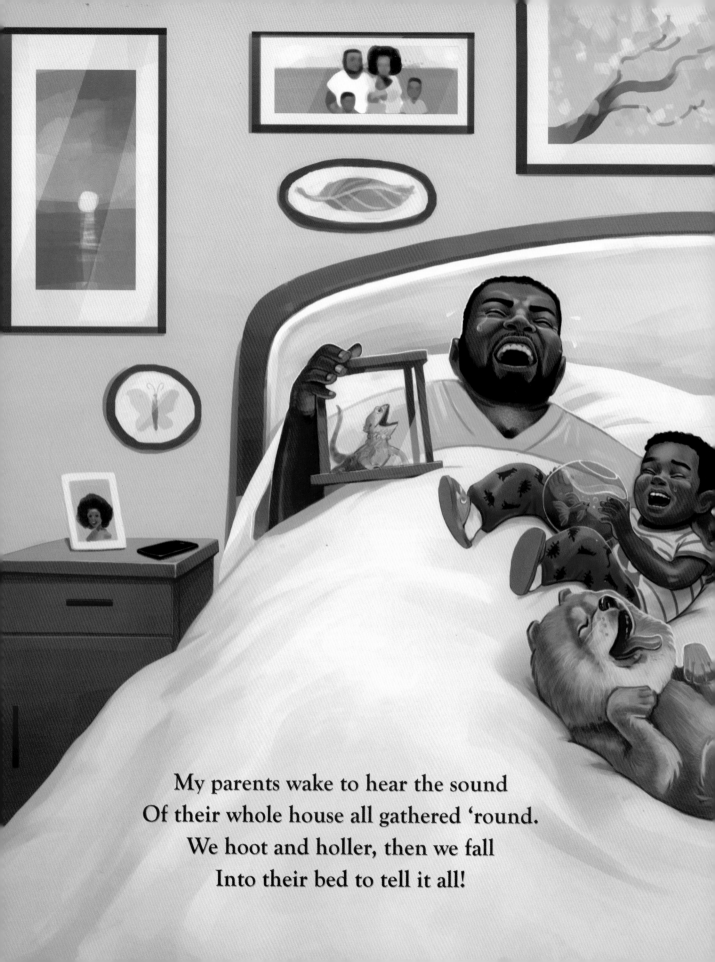

My parents wake to hear the sound
Of their whole house all gathered 'round.
We hoot and holler, then we fall
Into their bed to tell it all!

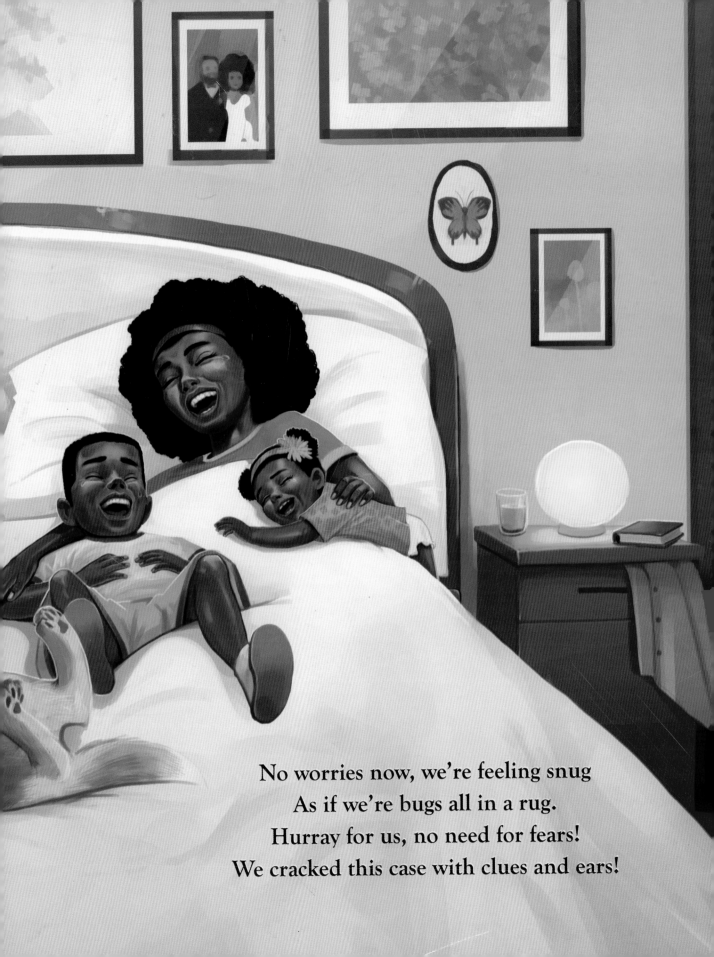

No worries now, we're feeling snug
As if we're bugs all in a rug.
Hurray for us, no need for fears!
We cracked this case with clues and ears!

ABOUT THE AUTHOR

This raucous tale comes from the creative mind of first-time author, Courtney B. Dunlap. She smiles now, but as a kid, Courtney was a scaredy-cat and would never dream of exploring in the dark. She's got a hunch that amongst her younger readers, she's not alone.

For those whose childhoods are a faint memory, *The Rumble Hunters* might remind you of a time when you, too, heard your first curious bedtime sounds. This is why *The Rumble Hunters'* enchanting sense of childlike wonder will appeal to all.

Courtney is married to Curtis, the love of her life, who willingly endures her famously corny jokes. She has the great honor of homeschooling three of her four beautiful children! When she's not tackling lesson plans or chasing her (almost) toddler, Courtney writes curriculum for The Gospel Project for Kids with LifeWay Christian Resources. She is also a sometime blogger over at www.able2teach.com. You can also follow her on Instagram at the handle @courtney_b_dunlap.

Saying she's ecstatic about publishing her first picture book would be an understatement! She believes *The Rumble Hunters* will be the first of many that spark imaginations for generations to come. She hopes that with this book, children of all ages will go beyond their fears to see the world through new eyes!

ACKNOWLEDGMENTS

The fact that I have the privilege of even writing the words "thank you" in my own book is truly unreal. That's why I must first begin by saying no amount of thanks I could give would ever be able to fully express the gratitude that's welling up in my heart. But I will try.

Thank you to my loving, faithful, encouraging, and overall handsomely amazing husband who has pushed me to never sell myself short and make my dreams a reality. To my four little rabbits, your mommy prays you can always see yourselves in the books she writes, this is why I do what I do.

To my parents, you guys have given me so much to be successful in this life and for that I am forever grateful. To my amazing mother-in-law, thank you for the faithful love you continuously show us! Between you and my parents, we are never without encouragement, support, and the occasionally sweet weekend getaway! We love you guys!

To my siblings (both by blood and through marriage), I want to thank you all for the continuously hyped up text messages I can read over and over that keep me going. To Lex and Maggs, our group chat gives me so much life!

To my beautiful nieces and nephews, Auntie Co says "Thank you!" because now the world knows this is the name I prefer regardless of the "Aunt Courtney" title your parents keep trying to force on me!

To my AMAZING bffs and circle of ridiculously loving and supportive friends, how could I have ever gotten this far without you? I hate that simply because of word count I can't name you individually but I hope your initials will suffice: EO, JW, RB, FF, YM, TB, TJ, RW, TG, MC, SG, AW, WC, and AMK. Oh my gosh, if I missed anyone please feel free to block me on Facebook (just kidding)!

And though I'm trying not to shout too many folks out by name, I honestly would be remiss if I didn't acknowledge my friend Casey Potter (a writing and editing extraordinaire in her own right). She took my poorly written, no-rhyme-scheme-having first manuscript, and gave me the tools to be the writer I am today. Thanks girl!

There are so many others who have made my writing journey worth it all, thank you! To my publishing team at Mascot Books (kudos to Rachel Sutton by the way), thank you for making it all happen! To my brilliant illustrator, Nazar Horokhivskyi, you have made all that I saw in my head come to life on paper. You have a true gift, thank you!

And last, but certainly not least, to my Savior and God, the Lord Jesus Christ, I pray that if I put my "thank you" on repeat until forever, it might come close to being enough. I love you!